29 AUG 2019

For you and your little star – MS

For my lovely Bloomsbury ladies, Kayt, Fiz, Zoe and Emma – NO

Bloomsbury Publishing, London, New Delhi, New York and Sydney

First published in Great Britain in 2014 by Bloomsbury Publishing Plc
50 Bedford Square, London, WC1B 3DP

Text copyright © Mark Sperring 2014
Illustrations copyright © Nicola O'Byrne 2014
The moral rights of the author and illustrator have been asserted

A CIP catalogue record of this book is available from the British Library

ISBN 978 1 4088 4960 6 (HB)
ISBN 978 1 4088 4961 3 (PB)

Printed in China by Leo Paper Products, Heshan, Guangdong

1 3 5 7 9 10 8 6 4 2

All papers used by Bloomsbury Publishing are natural, recyclable products made from wood grown in well-managed forests.
The manufacturing processes conform to the environmental regulations of the country of origin

www.bloomsbury.com

BLOOMSBURY is a registered trademark of Bloomsbury Publishing Plc

My Little Star

Mark Sperring
Nicola O'Byrne

BLOOMSBURY
LONDON NEW DELHI NEW YORK SYDNEY

When the day is done,
and sleep draws near,

when the moon's aglow

and stars appear . . .

I'll whisper something crystal clear –
words meant just for you to hear.

Let's look up so you can see

exactly what you mean to me.

Stars only shine in the dark night sky,

but you'll always twinkle in my eye.

You'll always twinkle
day and night.

Diamond-dazzling,
moonbeam bright.

My little star, you are, you are.

You are my little star.

And though other stars
   may fade and wane.

My little star, you will remain.

You always light the darkest night,
my little tiger burning bright.

My little star, you are, you are.

You are my little star.

Some use the stars to wish upon
     and make their dreams come true.

          But I've got everything I need –
               a bright and shining . . . you!

So close your eyes and snuggle tight

and dream the sweetest dreams tonight.

My little star, you are, you are …
Goodnight, my little star.